WITHDRAWN

Distributed in the U.S. by Chronicle Books
First Edition
Printed in China

ISBN: 978-1-934706-79-4

1 3 5 7 9 10 8 6 4 2

Deborah Zemke

My FURRY Valentine

Blue Apple Books

How do
you say,
"Be my valentine"?

We say it with flowers.

We
say it....

We walk on
the beach . . .

wing in wing.

We say it
with spots.

We say it . . . .

in lights.

with the look in our eyes!

We go . . .

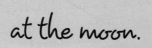

at the moon.

We love...

on a cruise.

beautiful
mooooosic.

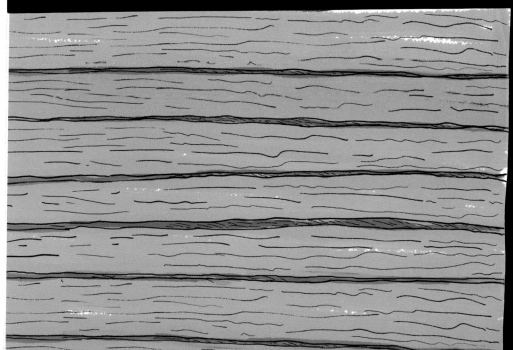

We croak in tune!

We shake . . . .

a tail feather.

We share . . .

ants!

nine lives together.

We join . . .

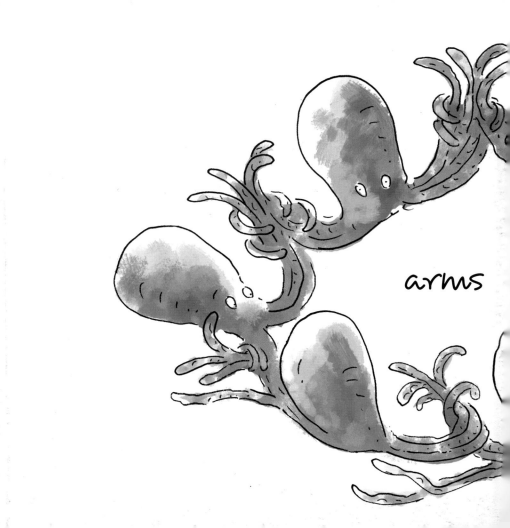

arms

and dance!

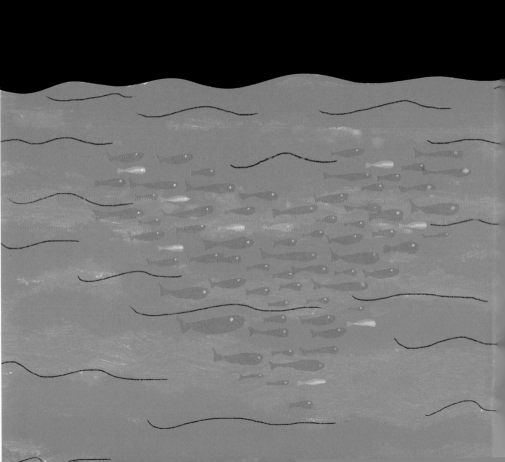

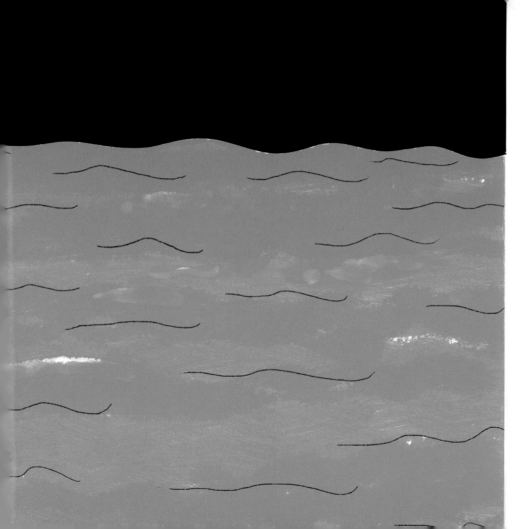

We
say it...

with
smiles.

in letters.

We fly...

thousands of miles . . .

to be home
together.

Be **sweet**...

be my furry valentine.